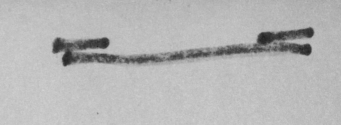

Which Pig Would You Choose?

by Edith Kunhardt

Greenwillow Books, New York

Magic Markers and a black pen were used
for the full-color art.
The text type is Egyptian 505 Roman.

Copyright © 1990 by Edith Kunhardt
All rights reserved. No part of this book
may be reproduced or utilized in any form
or by any means, electronic or mechanical,
including photocopying, recording or by
any information storage and retrieval
system, without permission in writing
from the Publisher, Greenwillow Books,
a division of William Morrow & Company, Inc.,
105 Madison Avenue, New York, N Y 10016.
Printed in Hong Kong by
South China Printing Company (1988) Ltd.
First Edition   10 9 8 7 6 5 4 3 2 1

Library of Congress Cataloging-in-Publication Data

Kunhardt, Edith.
Which pig would you choose? / Edith Kunhardt.
p. cm.
Summary: Maggie and Will spend a busy day on the farm,
making many choices in which the reader may share.
ISBN 0-688-08981-X (trade).
ISBN 0-688-08982-8 (lib. bdg.)
[1. Farm life—Fiction.   2. Literary recreations.]
I. Title.   PZ7.K94905Wk   1990
[E]—dc 19   88-35588   CIP   AC

TO AVA WEISS,

FOR HER PATIENCE

AND ENCOURAGEMENT

It was morning on the farm.

Maggie woke up.

Will woke up.

Maggie chose overalls.

Will chose jeans.

Which clothes would you choose?

Will liked oatmeal.

Maggie liked pancakes.

What do you like for breakfast?

Time to go out.

Maggie chose a straw hat.

Will chose a cap.

Which one would you choose?

Will and Maggie went to the barnyard.

Will carried a pail.

Maggie carried a bowl.

Which one would you carry?

Will fed the cow.

Maggie fed the chickens.

Which animal would you feed?

The mother pig had piglets.

Will liked the black piglet.

Maggie liked the spotted piglet.

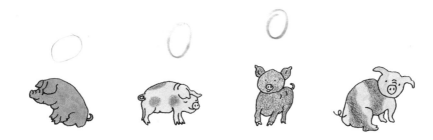

Which piglet do you like best?

Will rode on the tractor with Uncle Art.

Maggie rode on the horse with Aunt Stacey.

Which one would you like to ride on?

Will picked corn from the garden.
Maggie picked tomatoes.

Which vegetable would you pick?

Will and Maggie went home.

It was time for supper.

Maggie ate spaghetti with sauce.

Will ate spaghetti without sauce.

Which one would you eat?

Time for bed!

Will chose striped pajamas.

Maggie chose a pink nightgown.

Which one would you choose?

Good night, piglets.
Good night, chicks.
Sleep well, Maggie.
Sleep well, Will.

You sleep well, too.
Tomorrow you can choose again.

E
K

Kunhardt, Edith

Which pig would you
choose?

$12.88

DATE		

© THE BAKER & TAYLOR CO.